Giselle
the Christmas Ballet Fairy

To ballerinas everywhere

Special thanks to
Rachel Elliot

ORCHARD BOOKS
338 Euston Road, London NW1 3BH
Orchard Books Australia
Level 17/207 Kent Street, Sydney, NSW 2000
A Paperback Original

First published in 2014 by Orchard Books

© 2014 Rainbow Magic Limited.
A HIT Entertainment company.
Rainbow Magic is a trademark of Rainbow Magic Limited.
Reg. U.S. Pat. & Tm. Off. And other countries.

HiT entertainment

Illustrations © Orchard Books 2014

A CIP catalogue record for this book is available from the British Library.

ISBN 978 1 40833 377 8

1 3 5 7 9 10 8 6 4 2

Printed in Great Britain by CPI Group (UK) Ltd, Croydon, CR0 4YY

MIX
Paper from
responsible sources
FSC® C104740

The paper and board used in this paperback are natural recyclable products made from wood
grown in sustainable forests. The manufacturing processes conform to the environmental
regulations of the country of origin.

Orchard Books is a division of Hachette Children's Books, an Hachette UK company

www.hachette.co.uk

Giselle
the Christmas Ballet
Fairy

by Daisy Meadows

ORCHARD

www.rainbowmagic.co.uk

Jack Frost's Ice Castle

Well

Forget-me-not Glade

Rachel's House

Castle Springs Ballet School

Castle Springs Garden

Jack Frost's Spell

This ballet fairy know-it-all
Is in for a surprise.
When she sees Frostyev on stage,
She won't believe her eyes.

I'm the greatest! I'm the best!
But just to be quite certain,
I'll make all Christmas ballets fail
Before the final curtain!

The Magic Bottle

Contents

Best Friends Forever

"It's Christmas Eve," said Rachel Walker, gazing out of her bedroom window at the snowy sky. "Father Christmas and his elves are packing the sleigh full of toys, the reindeer are getting ready for their journey..."

"...And we are going to have the most amazing day ever," finished her best friend, Kirsty Tate.

Rachel turned and
smiled at her. The
one thing that
made Christmas
truly perfect
was being able
to share it with
each other. This
year was especially
exciting, because the girls had received
a wonderful early Christmas present.
Months ago they had entered a
competition called Best Friends Forever.
They had had to draw a picture of each
other and write one hundred words
about what made their best friend
special. They had forgotten all about the
competition until a typed white envelope
arrived, addressed to them both.

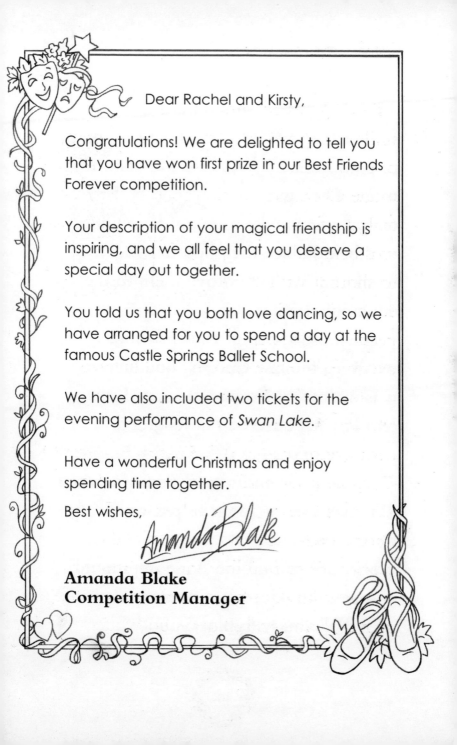

Dear Rachel and Kirsty,

Congratulations! We are delighted to tell you that you have won first prize in our Best Friends Forever competition.

Your description of your magical friendship is inspiring, and we all feel that you deserve a special day out together.

You told us that you both love dancing, so we have arranged for you to spend a day at the famous Castle Springs Ballet School.

We have also included two tickets for the evening performance of *Swan Lake*.

Have a wonderful Christmas and enjoy spending time together.

Best wishes,

Amanda Blake

Amanda Blake
Competition Manager

Rachel and Kirsty had got up early so that they would have plenty of time to pack their bags and decide what to wear. They were taking their ballet outfits, just in case they got the chance to dance. When they had finished breakfast, Mr Tate drove them to the dancing school.

The Castle Springs Ballet School was very famous, and the building was extremely old and elegant. Kirsty and Rachel gazed up at its grand entrance in awe.

"Have a splendid day," said Mr Tate. "I'll pick you up later, in plenty of time for the ballet."

The girls ran up the stone steps hand in hand. The door was open, and a huge hallway with black-and-white tiles stretched out in front of them. An enormous chandelier hung from the high ceiling, twinkling brightly, and a wide staircase curved up to the next floor.

"Oh my goodness," said Kirsty. "I've got butterflies in my stomach."

"Me too, a little bit," said Rachel with a nervous smile. "It's even more magnificent than I imagined."

Just then, a tall, willowy lady hurried towards them. She held out her arms and gave the girls a warm hug. Her silver hair was tied back in a loose ponytail, and her blue eyes sparkled.

"You must be Rachel and Kirsty," she said. "We've been looking forward to your visit very much. Congratulations on winning the prize. Friendship means a great deal to us here at Castle Springs. I am the director of the school, and my name is Sophia."

"We're really excited," said Kirsty.

"And a bit nervous!" added Rachel.

"Perhaps our prima ballerina can help calm your nerves," said Sophia, waving her arm towards the stairs.

A graceful, beautiful young woman was coming down the stairs, wearing a leotard and warm-up shorts. Her dark-brown hair was swept back under a hairband, and she smiled when she saw the girls.

"Hello, my name is Penny," she said.

Rachel and Kirsty felt very excited. They knew that the prima ballerina was the best and most important dancer in the company.

"It's lovely to meet you," said Kirsty. "We can't wait to see you dance."

"Well, I'm looking forward to seeing *you* both dance," said Penny. "I've arranged for you to attend the *corps de ballet* rehearsal class."

The girls were thrilled. The *corps de ballet* was the group of backing dancers in the ballet company. Lots of famous ballerinas had started their dancing careers in the *corps de ballet*. What amazing things would they learn in this class?

A Dancing Dream!

A short time later, Rachel and Kirsty were standing in a practice room with the members of the *corps de ballet*, who were chatting quietly. Penny was sitting on a wooden chair at the side of the room. The ballet mistress clapped her hands together and everyone fell silent.

"Good morning, everyone," she said, "and a special welcome to our guests, Rachel and Kirsty. I would like to start with a little introduction to the—"

She broke off to cough into her handkerchief.

"I'm sorry," she said with a croak in her voice. "As I was saying, I would like to give the girls a little introduction to the *corps de ballet*. Most great ballerinas started out in the *corps*. The dancers here are intelligent, hard-working, patient and disciplined. They share a group focus and they know how to work as a team."

She broke off to cough again, and Penny stood up.

"The *corps* is the heart of the company," she said. "If just one person forgets which arm to lift or which leg to stand on, it will spoil the whole scene. Together, these dancers can make or break a performance."

The ballet mistress smiled at her.

"So, without further ado, let's start our warm-up," she said. "First position, please. And, *demi-plié*."

Rachel and Kirsty followed the instructions as well as they could.

There were a few steps and positions
that they didn't know, but they were
surprised by how many they recognised.
The hardest part was keeping up – the
professional dancers were very fast.

"I feel as if my dancing is getting
better just from
watching them,"
Rachel
whispered
to her
best
friend.

"Me too,"
Kirsty
replied.
"Every
single one of
them is amazing!"

One of the dancers overheard and smiled at them.

"Just wait until you see Penny dance," she said. "It's like magic."

The girls smiled at each other. After all, they knew more about magic than most people! They had made friends with many fairies, and they loved sharing the secret of their exciting adventures.

After the warm-up, the class really began. Rachel and Kirsty tried to keep up, but the speed and variety of the moves was incredible. They couldn't manage all the jumps, and they hadn't expected the amount of acting the *corps* had to do. But it was very exciting to feel that for a short while they were swans, dancing under a magical spell.

At last the ballet mistress called a break.

"Take five minutes and have some water," she said in a rasping voice.

Rachel and Kirsty were very glad to have a chance to rest. They went back to the changing room to fetch their water bottles, chattering about all the things they had been doing.

"You must have to be able to learn really fast to be in the *corps*," said Kirsty. "There's so much to remember!"

"I'll be watching *all* the dancers at the performance tonight, just as much as the main ballerina," said Rachel, pushing open the changing-room door.

"Can you hear violins?" asked Kirsty suddenly.

Rachel listened and heard the faint sound of music.

"Do you think the class has started again already?" she asked.

Kirsty shook her head. "It sounds almost as if it's coming from your bag," she said.

"That's not possible," said Rachel, unzipping her bag to get her water. "OH!"

As soon as her bag was open, the girls heard a loud burst of vibrant string music, and then an exquisite fairy came pirouetting out towards them!

A Fairy and a Frosty Problem

For a moment, Rachel and Kirsty
just stared at the little fairy with their
mouths open. Even for a fairy, she was
so sparkly and beautiful that she almost
took their breath away. She was wearing
a glimmering silver leotard with a tutu,
and her satin ballet shoes were silver too.
Her chestnut-brown hair gleamed, and
her eyes were as bright as stars.

"Hello, Rachel
and Kirsty," said
the fairy. "I'm
Giselle the
Christmas
Ballet Fairy."

"Hello,
Giselle,"
said Kirsty.
"It's wonderful
to meet you —
especially here!"

Giselle looked around
and gave a merry laugh.

"Yes," she said, "this is the sort of place
where I belong, whether in the human
world or in Fairyland."

"You look like a prima ballerina," said
Rachel.

"I look *after* prima ballerinas," Giselle said with a smile. "I take care of all dancers who perform in Christmas ballets. It is the most special time of the year for ballet, because a good performance can take everyone who sees it on a magical journey."

"You must be very busy today, on Christmas Eve," said Kirsty.

"I should be watching over all the Christmas ballets and keeping the dancers safe and well," said Giselle.

"But Jack Frost has made up his mind to cause trouble for me this Christmas, and he's started by stealing my magic water bottle."

"Why does he want to cause trouble for you?" Rachel asked.

Giselle did an arabesque in mid-air.

"Ballet positions help me to think," she said, smiling. "I think Jack Frost is angry because I tried to give him some advice. He was dancing as Frostyev in his Goblinovski Festival

Ballet, and there were a few simple ways that he could have improved his style. I was trying to help, but he took it very badly. He said I was rude and interfering, and that he was going to get his own back."

"So he took your magic bottle," said Kirsty. "What does it do?"

"It makes sure that all ballerinas feel well before a performance," said Giselle. "Without it, winter coughs and colds could attack the dancers and spoil the Christmas ballets. I have no idea where Jack Frost has hidden it. Even Queen Titania's Seeing Pool hasn't been able to tell us anything. So she suggested that I came to ask for your help."

"Of course we'll help you," said Rachel.

At that moment they heard the ballet mistress calling everyone back in her croaky voice. The class was about to continue.

"You must finish your class," said Giselle. "I'll hide while you dance, and then perhaps we could search for Jack Frost afterwards?"

She slipped under Kirsty's ponytail and the girls ran to join the class. Most of the dancers were standing to one side of the room. Four ballerinas were in the centre, their arms crossed in front of one another, holding each others' hands.

"Ah, Rachel and Kirsty," said the ballet mistress. "We're going to rehearse a famous scene called *danse des petits cygnes*, which means the dance of the little swans."

The music began, and the four ballerinas began to dance sideways in a line, their legs and heads moving in unison.

"They will do sixteen *pas de chat*," the ballet mistress explained to the girls. "They must move at exactly the same time. The dance is meant to look like baby swans huddling together for protection."

"They make it look so easy," said Kirsty.

"That's their skill," said the ballet mistress, stifling a cough. "It is a tiring and challenging dance, but these girls have practised for months, and now they are perfect. Oh!"

The ballerina at one end of the line had stumbled and fallen!

Goblins in the Snow

The ballet mistress rapped her stick on the floor.

"Olivia, what's the matter?" she croaked.

Olivia blushed bright red.

"It's my feet, Madame," she said. "Suddenly it feels as if they're covered in blisters. It's too painful to dance."

"Go and treat them at once," said
the ballet mistress. "The opening
performance is just a few hours away,
and we have to be ready."

Olivia limped away and the rehearsal
continued with just three ballerinas. But
the music had hardly begun when the
middle dancer clutched her stomach and
groaned.

"Ooh, I've
got an awful
stomach ache!"
she cried.

"Go and lie
down, Samira,"
said the ballet
mistress.
"Where are the
understudies?"

Two other dancers stepped forward. As the ballet mistress was speaking to them, the dancer next to Kirsty suddenly staggered sideways.

"Are you all right?" asked Kirsty, holding her up.

"Dizzy," murmured the dancer. "Need air."

Rachel and Kirsty helped the fainting ballerina to the school's glass conservatory and lowered her onto a soft chair. Then they flung open the doors to the garden and let the cold, fresh winter air flow in.

The snow had stopped falling, and a few shafts of sunlight were breaking through the clouds.

"It's a pretty garden," said Rachel, looking out at the snow-covered hedges and arbours. "I bet it's full of roses in the summer."

Suddenly a distant sparkle caught their eye. At the far end of the garden was a pond, and two figures were bending over it, wrapped in fluffy white coats. Under Kirsty's ponytail, Giselle gave a little hop of excitement.

"Goblins!" she whispered. "Those are goblins, girls!"

The goblins were scooping up water from the pond and splashing each other.

Rachel looked down at her thin leotard and ballet shoes.

"We can't go outside dressed like this," she said. "But we *have* to find out what those goblins are doing here."

Kirsty glanced at the dizzy ballerina. She was bending forward with her eyes closed. Giselle slipped out of her hiding place and flicked her wand. A shower of silver sparkles landed on the girls, and instantly they found themselves wearing warm, fleecy jackets and wool-lined boots.

"Thank you!" whispered Kirsty.

They ran out of the conservatory and along the snowy path that led to the pond. Giselle fluttered between them. Now they were closer, they could see that the goblins were using drinking bottles to scoop up the water and squirt each other.

"Oh girls, those goblins have my magic bottle!" Giselle exclaimed.

Rachel marched up to the goblins and tapped them on the shoulders. They turned and then leapt into the air in shock.

"Go away!" they squawked. "Why are you poking your nose in here? Leave us alone!"

"Just give back the bottle that doesn't belong to you," said Rachel, holding out her hand.

"Oh, you mean *this* one?" asked the tallest goblin in a mocking voice.

He held up his bottle and threw it to the other goblin, who caught it and waved both bottles over his head.

"Or did you mean *my* bottle?" he asked with a snigger.

"Come on, humans, keep up!"

Kirsty had a sudden brainwave. She beckoned to Rachel and lowered her voice to a whisper.

"Giselle, can you use your magic to make more bottles?" she asked. "Perhaps we could try to confuse them."

Giselle performed a graceful *pas de chat* and, with a flick of her wand, a hundred identical bottles appeared on the path in front of them.

"Want to play?" said Rachel to the goblins.

She threw a couple of the bottles to the goblins, while Kirsty picked up three of them and started to juggle. The goblins tried to catch the new bottles and dropped them all.

"Butterfingers!" called Rachel. "Try again!"

She threw more bottles to the goblins… and more…and more. Then she started juggling too. Giselle used her magic to line the path with bottles. Soon there were so many bottles on the ground and in the air that the magic bottle had completely disappeared!

Bottle
Battle

"Stop!" the goblins screeched. "Where's our bottle?"

"It's *my* bottle," said Giselle, folding her arms and fluttering in front of them.

"But where *is* it?" asked Rachel.

With all the identical bottles on the ground, it was impossible to tell which was the magic one. The goblins

scrabbled around, trying to remember
which one it was. Rachel and Kirsty
exchanged confused glances. But Giselle
rose into the air and gazed down at the
scattered bottles. Then a swish of her
wand sent fairy dust sprinkling
down on all the bottles,
making them glow.
Most of the
sparkles faded,
but a bottle that
was lying on its
own underneath a
holly bush kept glowing.

"My bottle!" cried Giselle.

"Get it!" the tallest goblin squealed.

The goblins and Rachel ran for the
bottle, but Kirsty remembered a ballet
move that she had seen in the class.

She sprang through the air in a magnificent *jeté*. It looked as if she was doing the splits in the air!

She landed beside the bottle and picked it up, but the tallest goblin was already flinging himself at her. Kirsty threw the bottle as high into the air as she could.

"Giselle!" she cried.

Giselle zipped through the air and flung her arms around the bottle. Instantly, she and the bottle disappeared to Fairyland.

Rachel and Kirsty whirled around to face the goblins.

"It's gone," said Rachel. "Time to give up."

"Give it back!" the short goblin hollered. "Where have all the bottles gone?"

The girls looked around. The only bottle left was the ordinary one belonging to the goblins. The tallest goblin clutched his head with both hands.

"She's taken it!" he wailed. "What are we going to do?"

"We have to fake it," said the second goblin in a panicky voice. "Maybe if we glued some glitter on this bottle?"

They stomped off, talking about how to fool Jack Frost, and Rachel and Kirsty hugged each other.

"We did it!" said Rachel. "We found Giselle's magic bottle!"

"Do you think that means the ballerinas in our class will be feeling better?" Kirsty asked.

They hurried back into the school to find out. As soon as they were inside the conservatory, their magical boots and jackets disappeared, and they were back in their ballet outfits. The dizzy ballerina had gone, so the girls hurried back to the class. The music was playing and the dancers of the *corps* were busy rehearsing.

"Look," said Rachel. "All the ballerinas who felt ill are back! Oh Kirsty, it's worked!"

The ballet mistress waved at them.

"Come and join in, girls," she called. "Lots to get through! The dancers are practising the dance of the swans."

Her voice didn't sound croaky any more. The girls knew that Giselle's magic bottle must be protecting all ballerinas once again.

"I hope Jack Frost will leave Giselle

alone now," said Kirsty, as they went to join the ballerinas.

Rachel squeezed her hand. They both knew that Jack Frost didn't usually give up that easily.

"We'll be there to help Giselle if she needs us," she said. "And in the meantime, we've got a class to finish!"

The Ballet Bag

Contents

A Salad Thief

After the class, Rachel and Kirsty felt very hungry indeed. The *corps de ballet* rehearsal and the exciting adventure with Giselle had really worked up their appetites.

"Ooh, my stomach's rumbling," said Kirsty as she changed back into her ordinary clothes.

"It's nearly lunchtime," said Rachel, looking at her watch.

Just then, the ballerinas who had performed the dance of the little swans came up to them.

"Hi, I'm Olivia," said the dancer with red hair and freckles. "These are Samira, Alex and Ayesha. We were wondering if you'd like to have lunch with us in the canteen?"

"Thank you, we'd love to," said Kirsty with a smile.

The Castle Springs canteen was very different from the ones at Kirsty and Rachel's schools. Some people were dressed in ordinary clothes. Some were in tights and leotards. Others jostled past them in tutus and beautiful costumes, wearing tiaras and feathery plumes in

their hair. It was so interesting that the
girls kept staring and forgetting to eat.

"You're so lucky to be at such an
exciting school," said Kirsty to Ayesha.
Ayesha nodded and smiled.

"It *is* exciting," she said. "I feel very
lucky to be here and do something I love
so much every day. But it is very hard
work, and we don't have as much free
time as you do at an ordinary school.

We have to be careful to always eat healthy food, and we have to get up very early and go to bed early too."

"Do you ever get homesick?" asked Rachel.

"I did at first," said Alex. "It's strange to be living away from home. But I've made some really good friends here, and now we are in the *corps de ballet* there is no time to think about anything except *Swan Lake*!"

"We're really looking forward to the performance tonight," said Kirsty. "Are you feeling nervous?"

The four ballerinas exchanged glances and laughed.

"We're all very nervous indeed," said Samira. "But that's part of the life of a ballerina. I think that being nervous helps us to dance better, because we work so hard to get it right."

Everyone was looking at Samira as she spoke, but Rachel noticed something.

A small figure in a fluffy white coat was helping himself to the salad on Olivia's plate.

"Hey!" cried Rachel, half rising from her seat.

The figure scampered away, spitting out the salad and muttering, "Yuck! Healthy muck!"

Rachel and Kirsty exchanged glances.

"That was a goblin," Kirsty whispered as Rachel sat down again. "He was wearing the same coat as the ones we saw earlier in the garden."

"I wonder why he's still here," said Rachel. "I hope it doesn't mean more trouble for Giselle."

"Perhaps we should look for him after lunch," said Kirsty. "We could try to find out if he's up to mischief."

But before they could leave the table, the ballet school's prima ballerina, Penny, came to find them.

"I'd like to invite you to watch the principals rehearsing," she said.

Rachel and Kirsty gasped. They knew that the principals danced the most important parts in the ballet.

As they walked along beside Penny, she told them what to expect.

"I am dancing the lead role," she said. "That means that I appear as two different characters called Odette and Odile. Rupert Randall is dancing the role of Prince Siegfried."

Rachel remembered reading the story of *Swan Lake*.

"Prince Siegfried is in love with Odette, isn't he?" she asked.

"That's right," said Penny. "Odette is a princess who has been transformed into a swan by a sorcerer's magic spell, so she is dressed all in white. Odile is the daughter of the sorcerer, and she is magically disguised as Odette to trick Prince Siegfried. She is dressed all in black."

Rachel and Kirsty could hardly wait for the rehearsals to begin!

A Principal Problem

A short time later, Rachel and Kirsty were sitting on a bench at the side of the rehearsal room.

"The scene is a grand costume ball at the royal palace," said the ballet mistress. "Odile and Prince Siegfried dance together, and then the prince tells everyone that he wants to marry Odile."

The music began and Rupert Randall sprang into the centre of the room. He jumped so high that he almost seemed to be flying. Then Penny joined him. Standing on one leg, she whipped the other leg around, spinning on the spot.

"These are called *fouettés*," the ballet mistress told the girls. "Penny must do thirty-two

in a row. The people in the audience will be counting them, and they will

burst into applause when she finishes.
It is a very difficult step, and it shows a
ballerina's strength and skill."

But then something awful happened.
Penny wobbled, staggered sideways and
fell down with a loud bump. The music
stopped and everyone
stared at her in
shock.

"Are you all
right?" asked
Rupert,
helping her
to stand
up.

Penny
nodded,
but she looked
very upset.

"That has never happened before," she said. "I don't know what's wrong with me – I just couldn't remember what I was doing."

"Let's move on to another section," said the ballet mistress. "I'd like to see the *pas de deux* from Act Two, please."

Kirsty and Rachel knew that this was a scene where Prince Siegfried danced with Odette and fell in love with her. The music was slow and beautiful, and the dancing seemed perfect to the girls.

But the ballet mistress was frowning
as she watched. Then, as Rupert lifted
Penny above his head, his hands seemed
to slip on her waist. She fell, but luckily
she managed to land on her feet.

"I'm so sorry," said Rupert, looking
pale. "I just seemed to lose all strength in
my arms."

"You were both slightly out of
time with the music," said the ballet
mistress, looking worried. "There is a
tradition that a bad
rehearsal means
a good opening
performance. I
hope it's true!"

"Something
is wrong," said
Rachel in a low voice.

"Kirsty, let's slip out and look for that goblin. We have to find out if Jack Frost has something to do with this!"

When the girls returned to the canteen, it was empty. The kitchen area had been locked up behind shutters. The only sound they could hear was the faint music from different classes around the school.

"Perhaps he's gone back to the garden," said Kirsty.

They turned to leave, and then they heard a chair leg scraping on the wooden floor. "Someone's in here!"

Rachel exclaimed. "Quick, Kirsty, guard the door!"

Kirsty ran to the door and stood with her back to it. Now there was no way out. Rachel started to search the canteen, peering under tables and chairs.

"I know you're in here," she said. "Please stop hiding. We just want to talk to you."

Suddenly a table was shoved aside and the goblin sprinted away from Rachel towards the door. He skidded to a halt when he saw Kirsty.

"Get out of my way, you interfering human," he squawked. "You'll never find the ballet bag!"

"What do you mean?" asked Kirsty, as Rachel ran up to join her. "Whose ballet bag?"

"Mind your own business," said the goblin, poking out his tongue. "Jack Frost is much too clever for you and that silly ballet fairy."

He clamped his hand over his mouth, realising that he had said too much. Rachel folded her arms.

"So Jack Frost has stolen Giselle's ballet bag?" she asked. "Where is it?"

The goblin shook his head, still with his hand over his mouth. Kirsty turned to Rachel and gave her a secret wink. "There's no point asking him, Rachel," she said. "He doesn't know anything about the ballet bag."

"Oh yes I do," burst out the goblin in an offended voice. "I know everything."

The girls felt excited. Their plan was working – the goblin was getting annoyed. But could they make him tell them what had happened to the bag?

A Trip to Fairyland

"Jack Frost wouldn't have told a little goblin like you where he is keeping the bag," said Rachel.

"He didn't have to tell me," said the goblin in a boastful voice. "I was there with him when he threw it down the well."

"But I bet you don't know how to find the well," said Kirsty. "Jack Frost wouldn't trust you with that sort of important information."

"It's the well in the middle of Forget-me-not Glade, *actually*," said the goblin. "So there!"

Rachel and Kirsty smiled at each other.

"Well, you certainly showed us," said Rachel. "Sorry for not believing you."

They opened the door and the goblin stalked out with his nose in the air. As soon as he was out of sight, the girls hugged each other and jumped up and down in excitement. They had got the information they needed!

"Now we have to find Giselle and tell her about the bag," said Kirsty.

They opened the lockets they always
wore around their necks. Each one
contained a little fairy dust – just enough
to transport them to Fairyland. They
each took a pinch and sprinkled it over
themselves. It glittered
a dazzling silver
colour and then
– whoosh
– they had
shrunk to
fairy size.
Gossamer
wings unfurled
on their backs,
and a swirling cloud
of fairy dust lifted them off their feet.
The sparkles surrounded them like a
whirlwind.

"We're on our way to Fairyland!" cried Rachel.

A few seconds later, the girls were blinking in the bright sunshine. They were fluttering above the garden of the Fairyland Palace. Below, a stage had been set up in the middle of the garden. There was a semicircle of six golden chairs in front of the stage, padded with red plush velvet. Six fairies were sitting on the chairs. The girls recognised them all – Darcey the Dance Diva Fairy, Sophia the Snow Swan Fairy, Holly the Christmas Fairy, Kate the Royal Wedding Fairy, Eva the Enchanted Ball Fairy and Miranda the Beauty Fairy. The king and queen were on their thrones behind the golden chairs.

"Look, there's Giselle!" said Rachel.

The Christmas Ballet Fairy was
standing on the stage beside Bethany
the Ballet Fairy. They were talking with
their heads close together.

"Everyone looks worried, don't they?"
said Kirsty.

"Let's go down and tell them our

news," Rachel suggested. "Come on!"

They flew down and landed in front of the king and queen, dropping into low curtseys. Queen Titania smiled and rose to her feet.

"Quiet, please everyone," she said in her gentle voice. "We have some very important visitors."

Giselle flew down from the stage and landed beside the girls, hugging them tightly.

"I'm so happy to see you," she said.

"Thank you for helping me to find my magic bottle this morning."

"You're welcome," said Rachel, hugging her in return. "Are you putting on a performance?"

"It's a special preview of the Christmas ballet for the king and queen and a few of our dance-loving friends," Giselle explained. "It's the main performance tonight. But something has gone wrong, and I can't understand it. My solo was a disaster."

"Giselle tripped up and forgot her steps," said Queen Titania. "I have a feeling that something is very wrong, and I suspect that Jack Frost is behind it. You may have arrived just in the nick of time, Rachel and Kirsty. Perhaps you can help Giselle to investigate."

"We can do better than that!" said Kirsty. "There was a goblin in the Castle

Springs ballet school, and he told us that
Jack Frost has stolen Giselle's ballet bag."

All the other fairies had gathered
around to listen, and they started to gasp
and chatter. Giselle looked shocked.

"My ballet bag makes sure that all
rehearsals go well," she said. "Without
it, all this evening's performances will
be spoiled."

Forget-me-not Glade

"Girls, it is very important that we find the bag," said Queen Titania. "Could you help Giselle to look for it?"

"We know where it is!" said Rachel, squeezing Giselle's hand. "We tricked the goblin into telling us. Jack Frost has thrown it into a well in the middle of Forget-me-not Glade."

Giselle gave a puzzled frown, and looked around at the other fairies. Bethany shrugged, and the six fairy guests shook their heads.

"Are you sure that was the name?" asked Sophia. "I've never heard of it."

"That's what the goblin said," Kirsty replied. "Oh no, do you think he was fooling us?"

"I think that the goblin was telling the truth," said the queen, turning to the frog footman Bertram. "Please go to the ancient library and bring me the oldest map of Fairyland."

In a short time, Bertram came back with a large scroll of yellowing paper. It was covered in dust, and it looked very old. Two other frog footmen carried a table between them.

"Thank you," said the queen, taking the scroll.

She blew the dust away and unrolled the paper on the table. Rachel, Kirsty and all the fairies gathered around in excitement. The ink had faded with age, but it was clearly an ancient map of Fairyland.

Using one slender finger to search across the map, the queen began to explain.

"Many years ago, the Fairyland Palace

was surrounded by a large forest," she said. "There were hundreds of glades and pools and secret clearings – and fairies used them for dances and feasts and relaxation. Ah yes, it is as I thought."

The queen's finger stopped over a little glade in a valley, and everyone peered closer. The swirly writing beside the glade was faint, but Rachel and Kirsty could just make out the words.

Forget-me-not Glade

"That's it!" cried Giselle, performing a joyful *arabesque*. "That's where Jack Frost has hidden my ballet bag!"

"But how do we get there?" asked Kirsty. "The map is so old that Fairyland has changed a lot."

"The glade is in the same place," said the queen.

She waved her
wand, and
a piece of
paper fluttered
downwards into
Kirsty's hands.

"I have used a
navigation spell to
show you the way,"
said the queen. "Just
follow the arrows on the
paper, and they will take you there."

There was no time to lose. Waving
goodbye to their fairy friends, Rachel,
Kirsty and Giselle rose up into the
blue sky. Kirsty looked down at the
paper that the queen had given her,
and saw a green line appear with arrows
moving forwards.

"We have to go straight ahead," she said.

They zoomed off, following the moving arrows on the map. Kirsty kept checking it and telling Rachel and Giselle when they needed to fly left or right. They passed over tall trees and glittering pools. They crossed hills like small mountains. But at last they reached a place where the land dipped down into

a valley, and the arrows guided them
down among a little wood of pine trees,
tipped with snow. They landed on the
edge of a snow-covered meadow at the
heart of the wood. It was edged with
baby pine trees, and there was a little
stone well in the centre.

"Oh no," Rachel said with a groan. The well was guarded by two goblins!

A Squabble and a Dance

The goblins were squabbling fiercely, and the fairies strained to hear what they were saying.

"But it's *my* turn to see Frostyev and the Goblinovski Festival Ballet," the skinny goblin wailed. "It's a one-off performance!"

"You don't know anything about ballet," said the second goblin, who had a little pot belly. "I'm an expert, so I should be the one to go."

"Why can't we just both go?" complained the skinny goblin.

"You know why!" squawked the second goblin. "Jack Frost ordered us to always leave one guard here, and that should be *you*."

"You!" screeched the skinny goblin.

"You!"

"*You!*"

The goblins were standing on opposite sides of the well, glaring at each other. The fairies could not fly into the well without being seen. Giselle looked up at the sky, and saw that the sun was beginning to set.

"We have planned our Christmas ballet for this evening," she said. "Without my ballet bag it will be hopeless, and time is running out."

"I've got an idea," said Kirsty. "We need to distract the goblins, and it sounds as if they both love ballet. Giselle, could you do a dance for them?"

A little smile replaced Giselle's worried frown.

"I don't think they would want to see a fairy dance," she said. "But I think that some of these trees might be able to help."

She waved her wand towards the baby trees that surrounded the glade. Fairy dust flew from the tip and swirled upwards. Some of it sprinkled down on the trees, while the rest turned into musical notes that hung in the air. Enchanting music began to play – faintly at first, and then gradually getting louder. The goblins stopped squabbling.

"Can you hear that?" asked the one

with the pot belly.

"Sounds like ballet music," said the skinny one.

Then their mouths dropped open. All around the glade, the baby trees began to sway to the music. They glided forwards through the snow, reaching up their delicate branches like arms and shaking white snowflakes all around them.

The goblins stared in wonder as the trees twirled and swayed around them. The music grew louder and the goblins stepped away from the well, clasping their hands together as they gazed at the trees. They didn't see that Giselle was hovering on the edge of the glade, directing the trees with her wand like an orchestra conductor.

"Now's our chance!" she whispered to Rachel and Kirsty.

Rachel instantly zoomed towards the well and flew down into the darkness. Kirsty waited, holding her breath.

The seconds ticked
by. Then, just when
she thought that
something must have
gone wrong, Rachel
shot out of the well
with the ballet bag
clutched in her arms.

The enchanted music
ended at once, and the trees slid back to
their places. Puzzled, the goblins looked
around and saw the three fairies.

"Go away!" screeched the skinny
goblin.

"You can't have the bag," said the
second goblin, blowing a raspberry at
them.

"We've already got it," said Rachel,
handing the bag to Giselle.

Horrified, the goblins let out wails of rage.

"You tricksy fairies!" shrieked the goblin with the pot belly. "You'll be sorry! Jack Frost will get his own back on you!"

They trudged off through the snow, and Rachel and Kirsty turned to Giselle.

"What do you think they meant by that?" asked Kirsty.

"Don't worry," said Giselle in an airy voice. "There is nothing that Jack Frost can do to me now.

As long as my silver ballet shoes are safe, everything will be all right. And my ballet shoes are under guard in the palace, so nothing can possibly go wrong."

Giselle tapped the girls' lockets with her wand and filled them with fairy dust again. Then she smiled at both girls.

"You have saved tonight's performances," she said. "Thank you from the bottom of my heart. Now it is time for me to send you home so that you can enjoy *Swan Lake*."

Rachel and Kirsty were very happy to have been able to help Giselle again. But they couldn't help wondering what Jack

Frost would say when he heard about
the ballet bag!

The Silver
Ballet Shoes

Contents

Backstage at the Ballet

"I can't remember the last time I've had such a busy day," said Rachel. "We've watched the rehearsals for *Swan Lake*, and we've helped Giselle get back her magic water bottle and ballet bag from Jack Frost."

"The day isn't over yet," said Kirsty. "We've still got this evening's performance of *Swan Lake* to watch. I can't wait!"

The best friends were standing backstage, watching the dancers and crew prepare for the ballet. During their day at the Castle Springs Ballet School they had made friends with the prima ballerina, Penny. She had said that they could stay backstage until just before the ballet began.

It was very exciting to be backstage. Kirsty and Rachel stood out of the way and watched as dancers dashed past in a flurry of tutus and feathery costumes. The props manager was preparing everything the dancers would need, and the wardrobe mistress was following the ballerinas around with a needle and thread, making last-minute alterations and repairs. The lighting was dim, but everywhere they looked the girls could see the sparkle of glitter on tutus and diamonds on tiaras.

"The stage is just over there," said Kirsty, pointing to the right. "Shall we go and have a look at the scenery for the first act?"

"Ooh yes, let's!" said Rachel at once.

They tiptoed onto the stage. Thick velvet curtains hung between them and the audience, but they could hear the shuffle of hundreds of feet and the rustle of theatre programmes. Above the hum of chatter from the crowd, the girls could also hear the squeaks, toots and pings of the orchestra tuning up their instruments.

The scenery showed the garden
of a royal palace. Roses, lilies and
trees surrounded a sunny courtyard,
while the palace in the distance was
gleaming white.

"The theatre's painters must be so artistic," said Kirsty. "I thought it wouldn't look as pretty up close as it does when you're in the audience, but it's perfect."

She traced over a picture of climbing pink roses with her finger. She could see every thorn and petal.

"I suppose it has to look beautiful for the dancers too," said Rachel. "Oh, that's lovely!"

She picked up a golden bow, which was lying on a white table.

"That's the present that the queen gives to the prince in the first act," said Kirsty, remembering the start of the story.

Rachel rose onto her toes and raised her leg behind her, as she had seen the prince do in rehearsals. Then she lifted the bow above her head. There was a musical twang and a golden arrow flew into the air.

"Oh!" Rachel exclaimed. "How did that happen? I didn't do it!"

The arrow fell back down towards them, shining like a golden wand.

"That's not an arrow," cried Kirsty. "It's Giselle!"

The Christmas Ballet Fairy was pirouetting downwards, her wand raised above her head.

"Oh girls," said Giselle, holding out her arms to them. "I'm sorry to interrupt your evening, but I've got some terrible news!"

Goblins and Guards

"What's happened?" asked Rachel.

"I bet it's got something to do with Jack Frost," said Kirsty.

"You're right," Giselle replied. "I should have paid more attention to the goblins' warning, but I was so sure that my silver ballet shoes were safe in the palace. While we were warming up

for the Christmas ballet performance,
Jack Frost and his goblins arrived at
the palace. I'll show you exactly what
happened."

She waved her wand, and a shimmery
moving picture appeared on the red
stage curtain. It looked as if someone
was projecting a film onto the velvet.
The girls could see four mice standing
guard outside a large wooden door. The
guards looked very serious and smart.
Each one was wearing a tunic of red
and gold, with a brown belt around
the middle. From each belt hung a
golden horn. On their heads the
mice were wearing three-cornered red-
and-gold hats.

As Rachel and Kirsty watched, a
gaggle of goblins scampered up to the

guards. They were all wearing tutus, squawking and shouting. They leapt up and down in front of the guards, waving their arms and trying to pull off the three-cornered hats.

"Catch them!" ordered one of the guards.

At this, the goblins scattered in all directions and the guards chased after them. While the door was unguarded, Jack Frost tiptoed up to it. None of the guards saw him – they were too busy trying to control the goblins. Jack Frost pointed his wand at the lock, and the door swung open. He crept inside, and came out a few seconds later with a pair of shining silver ballet shoes in his hand.

"Frostyev and the Goblinovski Festival Ballet will dance again tonight!" he cackled.

134

The picture faded as Giselle turned to look at the girls.

"Those are my magical ballet shoes," she said, her wings drooping slightly. "As soon as we heard what had happened, the king and queen sent the Dance Fairies to the Ice Castle, but there was no one there. We have no idea where to look, and Christmas ballets everywhere are about to start. As long as Jack Frost has my magic shoes, all ballets will be ruined. What shall we do?"

Before the girls could reply, they heard cries and shouts from the side of the stage.

"Something's wrong," said Rachel. "Come on!"

Giselle tucked herself under a lock of Rachel's hair and the girls hurried to see what all the shouting was about. They found the director surrounded by dancers and backstage crew, all looking angry and upset.

"Who has taken my costume?" the dancer playing the queen was wailing.

"My shoes are stained!" one of the younger ballerinas cried out.

"My props box is all muddled!" a stagehand was shouting.

"Half the swans' tutus are missing," complained the wardrobe mistress.

The director held up her hands and then put them over her ears.

"Please, stop shouting!" she said. "This is a disaster! Why is everything going wrong? Everyone must start searching the dressing rooms, from the stagehands to the prima ballerina herself. Hurry! If these problems aren't sorted out in the next half hour, I am going to have to cancel the performance."

Rachel and Kirsty exchanged looks of alarm.

"We can't let that happen," Kirsty said in a determined voice. "So many people have been looking forward to this ballet."

"Including us," added Rachel. "Christmas Eve will be ruined unless we

can get the silver ballet shoes in the next
half hour!"

Frostyev Onstage

Rachel and Kirsty hurried down dimly lit corridors until they reached the dressing rooms. All the doors were open, and people were rushing in and out of the rooms in panic.

"Just keep looking, everyone!" the wardrobe mistress said, hurrying along behind the girls. "We must find those missing costumes."

"Can we help?" Kirsty asked her.

But the wardrobe mistress didn't hear

her. She swept
past the girls
and started
rummaging
through
a rail of
tutus in the
corridor.
Rachel took
a step forward
to try to get her
attention.

"Wait," said Kirsty, grabbing Rachel's arm. "Look!"

Someone in a tutu was just disappearing around the end of the corridor.

"That's odd," said Rachel. "Who could be leaving when the director has ordered everyone to stay here and search the dressing rooms for the missing tutus?"

"Let's find out," said Kirsty.

The girls hurried along the corridor, but when they turned the corner they only caught a glimpse of the mystery dancer's tutu as it disappeared around another corner. On and on the dancer led them, turning left and right through the maze of backstage corridors.

"I think we're heading back towards the stage," said Rachel eventually.

They rounded another corner and arrived back beside the stage. The curtain was still down, but the stage was now filled with a flurry of dancers in sparkling white tutus. They were rehearsing, but they were not ordinary ballerinas. The legs that stretched out behind them were green, and their heads were bald underneath their glimmering tiaras. They were goblins!

"It's the Goblinovski Festival Ballet – Jack Frost's ballet company!" said Kirsty. "They're here!"

"And they're wearing the missing tutus," Rachel added.

Giselle peered out from underneath Rachel's hair.

"That's not all," she said in a low voice. "Jack Frost is here too – as Frostyev!"

Through a gap in the crowd of goblin dancers, they could see Frostyev standing on one leg, with the other leg pointing straight up in the air. He was wearing a tight silver costume and there were silver spangles in his hair and beard. "I'm the best dancer in the world!" he declared, cackling with laughter. "And the cleverest, too!"

"Dance some more! Dance some more!" squealed the goblins, clapping their hands together and jumping up and down.

Frostyev pirouetted across the stage with his arms above his head. Even though Rachel and Kirsty were worried, they couldn't help noticing that he was dancing very well.

"While those stupid fairies are searching for me at the Ice Castle, I'll be giving a gaggle of silly humans the performance of a lifetime," Frostyev told the goblins. "They'll all be talking about me. No one will ever want to see another dancer, because I am so perfect and such an icy genius!"

"What if the humans are too stupid to know that you're so brilliant?" asked one of the goblins.

Frostyev stopped pirouetting and scowled. "If they don't clap then I will have the fun of turning them all into toads!" he snapped.

He sprang into the air so high that he seemed to be flying. His feet were beside the goblins' heads, and Giselle gave a horrified gasp.

"He's wearing my silver ballet shoes!" she cried. "That's why his dancing is so perfect. Nothing can stop him now!"

An Unexpected Interview

The goblins were getting bored
of listening to Frostyev's boasting.
Three of them hurried over to the red
velvet curtain.

"Let's peek at the audience and pull
faces at them," suggested a short goblin
with dirt on his face.

They huddled together and peered
underneath the curtain.

"Oh dear, I hope no one spots them," said Kirsty. "I'm sure I heard that there are going to be some journalists and ballet critics here tonight. It would be terrible if a photo of the goblins got into the newspapers."

"Oh!" Rachel exclaimed. "That's given me an idea. Giselle, could you disguise us as journalists? If we can flatter Frostyev and distract him, we might be able to get your shoes back."

"Oh, yes, please try!" said Giselle, clasping her hands together.

A few moments later, Rachel and
Kirsty walked onto the stage looking
very different indeed. Rachel was
wearing sunglasses and had a camera
slung around her neck. Her hair was
hidden under a pink beret. Kirsty's hair
was piled up on top
of her head and
decorated with
sparkling
butterfly
clips. She
was wearing
a purple
jumpsuit with
strings of beads
around her neck,
and carrying a
notebook and pen.

Frostyev stopped
dancing and
glared at them.

"Who are
you?" he
demanded
in a rude
voice.

"Ooh, it's
really him!"
exclaimed Rachel, putting her hand over
her heart. "The one and only Frostyev!
I'm so excited I can hardly breathe!"

"We're from *Exclusively Ballet*, the
bestselling ballet magazine," said Kirsty,
holding out her hand. "We're longing to
interview you for our next issue, because
you're the most magnificent dancer we
have ever seen."

Frostyev gave a smug little smile and shook her hand.

"Your sales will double with a picture of *me* on the cover," he said.

"Our readers will want to know everything about you," Rachel added. "How do you leap so high? How do you stay so handsome?"

"Well…" said Frostyev.

"What are your beauty secrets?" Kirsty went on. "Where do you have your beard trimmed?"

"I have never—" Frostyev began.

"And of course the most interesting question of all," said Rachel, talking over him. "*Why* do you tie your ballet shoe ribbons in such an old-fashioned way?"

Frostyev drew himself up to his full height and narrowed his eyes.

"What do you mean, 'old-fashioned'?" he demanded in a huffy voice. "I'm the latest and the greatest, and don't you forget it. I'm the freshest, most up-to-date dancer in the whole world."

"But none of the modern ballet dancers tie their ribbons that way," said Kirsty, pointing to the silver ribbons criss-crossing his feet. "I'll show you the new way if you like."

"Yes, do it right now," Frostyev ordered. "I can't perform if I look unfashionable."

He sat down and stuck out his legs. Kirsty crouched down beside him and Rachel crossed her fingers behind her back. Would her best friend be able to untie the shoes before Frostyev realised who they really were? Working quickly,

Kirsty untied the long silver ribbons.
Frostyev was expecting her to re-tie
them, so this was the most dangerous
moment of the plan. She had to be fast!

Everyone's Perfect Christmas

Kirsty tried to pull the shoes off gently, so that Frostyev wouldn't notice. But they were clamped tightly around his bony feet, and he frowned down at her.

"What are you doing?" he asked, bringing his face closer to hers.

Kirsty shivered as she looked into his cold, pale eyes.

"Wait a minute, I recognise you!" he exclaimed.

"Kirsty, quickly!" cried Rachel.

With a hard tug, Kirsty yanked the ballet shoes from Frostyev's feet. He threw himself at her, but she just had time to hurl the shoes into the air as he knocked her backwards.

Giselle zoomed out of the shadows
and grabbed one of the shoes,
while Rachel
leapt up to
catch the
other. She
handed it
to Giselle,
and the shoes
instantly shrank to
fairy size. At the
same moment,
the tutus and
tiaras vanished from the goblin dancers.
Rachel and Kirsty smiled at each other.
Everything was returning to normal.

A flurry of sparkling fairy dust
surrounded Frostyev, and a few seconds
later his ballet costume had disappeared.

He was Jack Frost again. He scrambled
to his feet and shook his fist at them all.

"Give me back those shoes!" he bawled
at Giselle, who was fluttering above his
head.

"Certainly
not," she
replied. "They
are my shoes
and you
stole them.
You have
been very
mean,
trying to
spoil the fun
of Christmas
ballets, but it hasn't
worked – thanks to Rachel and Kirsty."

The little fairy smiled at the girls, whose journalist disguises had now disappeared.

"But what am I supposed to do?" Jack Frost demanded. "The Goblinovski Festival Ballet can't perform now."

"Go back to your Ice Castle where you are needed," said Giselle in a gentle voice. "It's winter time, and your snow and ice are very important."

Jack Frost stared at her for a moment, and then raised his wand in the air.

"Come on, you nincompoops," he snapped at the goblins. "There's work to be done. Stop messing around here and come with me!"

The goblins gathered around him.

"Merry Christmas, Jack Frost," said Giselle.

For a moment, a little smile hovered around Jack Frost's mouth.

"Merry Christmas," he said in a gruff voice.

There was a bright blue flash, and then Jack Frost and his goblins vanished from the stage. All that remained were a few melted snowflakes, which Giselle dried up with a wave of her wand.

"Thank you, Rachel and Kirsty," she said. "Now I can make sure that tonight's performances are a huge success.

I must return these shoes to Fairyland in time for curtain up. Merry Christmas to you both!"

"Merry Christmas, Giselle!" called the girls.

As the little fairy disappeared, the director hurried onstage towards the girls.

"Good news!" she said. "All the costumes have been found! Hurry to your seats now, girls – the ballet is about to start."

Kirsty and Rachel dashed to find their seats as the orchestra began to play the opening music. They saw their parents waving to them, and sat down just in time. The curtain rose to reveal a bustling birthday scene, with the handsome prince at the centre of the celebrations.

"This is going to be the ballet of the year!" Mrs Walker murmured to the girls.

"And a really magical end to our ballet adventures," Kirsty whispered. "Merry Christmas, Rachel."

"Merry Christmas, Kirsty," Rachel replied. "I'll never forget a single moment!"

Now it's time for Kirsty and Rachel to help...

Heidi
the Vet Fairy

Read on for a sneak peek...

Rachel Walker opened her eyes and saw the early-morning sun making shadow patterns on the ceiling. For a moment she couldn't think why she felt so excited. Then she remembered. Today, she and her best friend Kirsty Tate were going to work in a vet's surgery. She sat up and looked across the room. Kirsty was still fast asleep in her bed.

"Wake up, Kirsty!" said Rachel, swinging her legs out of bed. "I can't wait to see all the animals!"

Kirsty sat up and rubbed her eyes. Then she gave a huge smile.

"I was dreaming that we were vets," she said. "Today is going to be so much fun!"

Rachel was staying with Kirsty for half term, but they hadn't expected her visit to be quite so exciting. On the first day of the holiday, Kirsty's next-door neighbour Lisa had popped round to ask them an important favour.

Lisa was a vet, and she had just opened her own surgery in the village. She had arranged for some local journalists to come for an open day, so they could write reviews in their papers. She was hoping that they would say good things in their reports so that people would bring their animals to her.

Lisa had asked Rachel and Kirsty if

they would help her out on the open day. They were going to look after the journalists as they looked around the surgery. The girls would be making cups of tea and coffee, serving sandwiches and other refreshments, and keeping the waiting rooms nice and tidy.

"It was kind of Lisa to have uniforms made in our size," said Rachel as she pulled on the blue shirt with its white logo. "We're really going to look like part of the team."

"I think that being a vet must be one of the best jobs in the world," said Kirsty. "I'd love to spend every day helping poorly animals get well again."

"I hope that the journalists say good things about Lisa's surgery," said Rachel. "It's very useful to have a good vet nearby."

She stroked Kirsty's pet cat, Pearl, who gave a loud purr.

"Pearl agrees!" said Kirsty with a laugh.

"I hope that we get to spend some time with the animals too," said Rachel. "I wonder what different sorts of pets we'll meet."

"A kangaroo would be fun!" said Kirsty.

"Or a dolphin," said Rachel, with a secret smile at her best friend.

Kirsty smiled back. She guessed that Rachel was remembering the wonderful adventure they had shared with Ally the Dolphin Fairy and her dolphin friend Echo. Ever since they had first met on Rainspell Island, they had made many fairy friends and had lots of happy adventures together.

After breakfast, the girls pulled on their shoes and hurried next door. Lisa answered their knock.

"Good morning, girls!" she said in a cheerful voice. "Are you looking forward to today?"

"Very much!" said Rachel with a big smile.

Read Heidi the Vet Fairy to find out what adventures are in store for Kirsty and Rachel!

Join in the magic online by signing up
to the Rainbow Magic fan club!

Meet the fairies, play games and
get sneak peeks at the latest books!

There's fairy fun for everyone at

www.rainbowmagicbooks.co.uk

You'll find great activities, competitions, stories and
fairy profiles, and also a special newsletter.

Find a fairy with
your name!